WHEN
Virona the Corona
CAME TO TOWN

WRITTEN & ILLUSTRATED
BY: HAILEY GLYNN

To my mother, Trish Glynn:

Thank you for being my rock & inspiring me to become an author! **I love you!**

All inquires about this book can be sent to the author at
growingwithglynn@gmail.com
Published in the United States
ISBN: 9798645549046
For more information visit my website:
www.growingwithglynn.org

This book belongs to:

_____

_____

During the Coronavirus Pandemic
I was _____ years old. I spent my
time_____. I was
quarantined with _____.

Virona the Corona just showed up one day,
and it looked like she was here to stay.
Her first stop was **Wuhan** to say nihao,
then off to **Italy** to yell ciao.

Leaving **destruction**
in her path,
Virona wanted everyone to
feel her **wrath**.
Across the pond and
to the states,
sparking fear. and
cancelling dates.

When **Virona** came to town
everything shut down.
If you went outside
there was no one around.
Humans stayed home
to get **Virona** to stop.
The dogs were **SO HAPPY**...
the cats were **NOT**!

MaryEllen woke up and
got ready for school.
Ready to learn and
follow the rules!
She put on her shoes and
tied her braid.
Little did she know,
it'd be her **last day** in
first grade.

Ms. Glynn
Rm. 107

Everything was changing and she missed her friends. MaryEllen just wanted this all to **end**. Restaurants closed and she had to eat mom's cooking... those brussel sprouts are **NOT** good-looking!

The next day **MaryEllen**
had to wear a **mask**.
She had so many questions to ask!
Why is **Virona** the Corona so **mean**?
Why do we have to keep
everything so **clean**?

Six feet apart and
signs on every door,
social distancing was the
new norm.
There were few things
that didn't **change**.
Everything just felt
so **strange**.

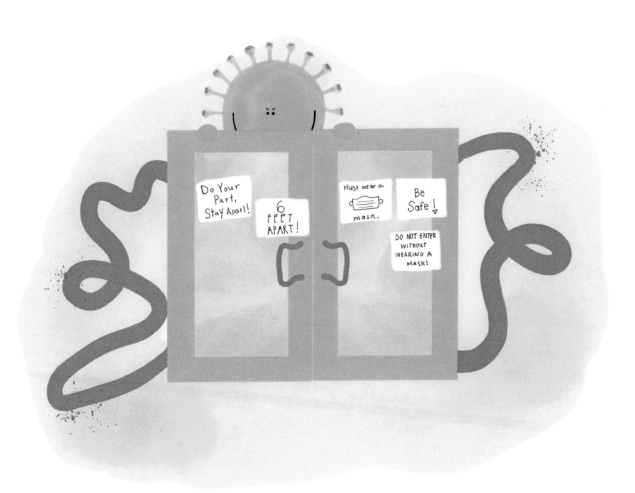

One day **Virona**
asked **MaryEllen** to play,
MaryEllen said **noooo** way!!!
She ran to the sink to
scrub **Virona** off.
She sang the **ABC's** twice and
escaped that awful cough.

Her **teacher** was the
hero who taught the ABC trick.
Virona was vicious, but
MaryEllen was quick!
MaryEllen thought of her teacher
just then,
wanting to show off her new
toothless grin!

She watched her teacher's lessons and had class **Zooms,** but it just wasn't the same as being in the **classroom.** She missed hearing her nickname, **"Smarty Bug,"** but most of all she missed bear **hugs.**

MaryEllen dreamed
of all the people she missed,
her **sisters** and **brothers**
were at the top of the list.
She couldn't see them and her
emotions swirled, but they were
out **saving the world**.

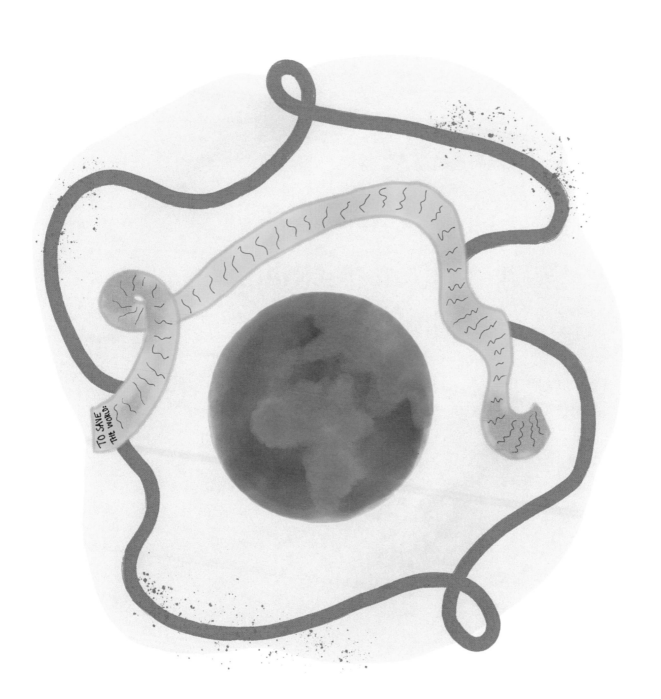

Her one sister, Sydney,
is a **nurse,**
an important **hero**
in our universe!
Her other sister, Nancy,
runs a **grocery store,**
she is a **hero**
to the core.

Her brother, Tom,
is a **first responder**.
'Could he be more amazing'
she began to ponder.
Her other brother, Jax,
was a **mailman**,
everyone should be his number
one fan!

MaryEllen was becoming sad on
this dreary day,
wondering if **Virona** the Corona
would ever go away.
But just then,
the **sun** started to come out.
MaryEllen looked up
and **reversed** her pout.

She started thinking,
maybe it's **not** all that bad...
She was able to spend **time** with her
moms and grandad.
She had fun **helping** her mom make
masks for others,
even if she missed her
sisters and brothers!

MaryEllen learned about **pollution**
and that it was getting a
little better.
She learned to **draw** a shark and
wrote her best friend a **letter**.
She knew for sure
Virona the Corona was **bad**...
but that didn't mean she always
had to be **sad**.

MaryEllen saw a rainbow
and ran out to play.
She wouldn't let this nasty virus
ruin her fun day.
She played a new game called
'strut, strut, strut',
where she kicked Virona's
butt, butt, butt!

Even when her world was turned
upside down, MaryEllen realized
she could always flip her frown.
When scary things happen,
show extra appreciation to others.
Here's a reminder to hug your
sisters and brothers!

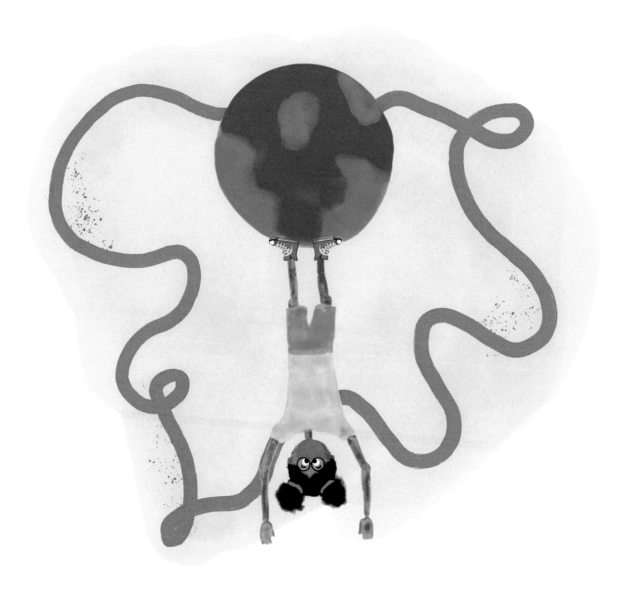

NOTE FROM THE AUTHOR

Hi! I'm Hailey, a first grade teacher in Buffalo, NY.
I hope you have enjoyed reading "When Virona the Corona Came to Town."
It is the first book I have written!
The goal of this story is to shed light on a time of extreme uncertainty and fear in a child-friendly way.
My hopes are to help children understand this unprecedented and historical time while learning to cope with difficult feelings. Moreover, I hope to spread appreciation for the heroes of this time and portray the power of a positive mindset.

Let's connect on Social Media : Growing With Glynn

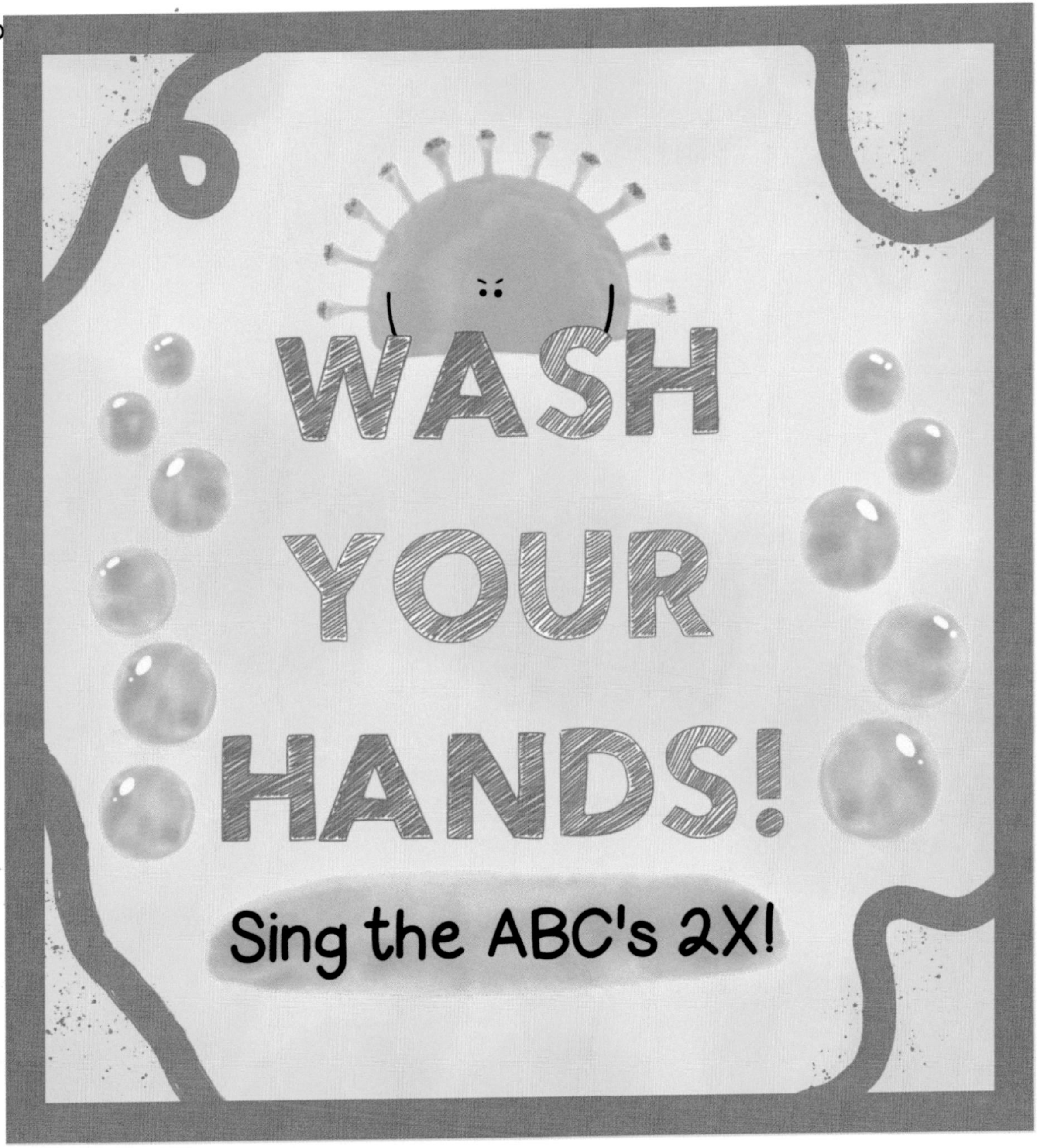
WASH YOUR HANDS!
Sing the ABC's 2X!

Made in the USA
Coppell, TX
23 August 2020